ARCTIC
ANIMALS
AT RISK

HARP
SEALS

JESSIE ALKIRE

**Checkerboard
Library**

An Imprint of Abdo Publishing
abdobooks.com

▶ ABDOBOOKS.COM

Published by Abdo Publishing, a division of ABDO, PO Box 398166, Minneapolis, Minnesota 55439. Copyright © 2019 by Abdo Consulting Group, Inc. International copyrights reserved in all countries. No part of this book may be reproduced in any form without written permission from the publisher. Checkerboard Library™ is a trademark and logo of Abdo Publishing.

Printed in the United States of America, North Mankato, Minnesota
102018
012019

 THIS BOOK CONTAINS RECYCLED MATERIALS

Design and Production: Mighty Media, Inc.
Editor: Liz Salzmann
Cover Photographs: Shutterstock
Interior Photographs: Alamy, pp. 5, 19; AP Images, p. 27; iStockphoto, pp. 12–13, 21, 29; Lysogeny/Wikimedia Commons, p. 25; Shutterstock, pp. 7, 9, 11, 14, 15, 16, 22–23, 28

Library of Congress Control Number: 2018948506

Publisher's Cataloging-in-Publication Data
Names: Alkire, Jessie, author.
Title: Harp seals / by Jessie Alkire.
Description: Minneapolis, Minnesota : Abdo Publishing, 2019 | Series: Arctic animals at risk | Includes online resources and index.
Identifiers: ISBN 9781532116964 (lib. bdg.) | ISBN 9781532159800 (ebook)
Subjects: LCSH: Harp seal--Juvenile literature. | Marine animals--Adaptation--Arctic regions--Juvenile literature. | Environmental protection--Arctic regions--Juvenile literature. | Habitat protection--Juvenile literature.
Classification: DDC 599.748--dc23

TABLE OF
CONTENTS

SEAL FIGHT!

Agroup of female harp seals are clustered together on the sea ice. Two male seals approach from opposite directions. Both male seals begin barking and chirping at one female. The males wave their fins and growl at each other. There is only one way to solve this matter. They prepare to fight for the right to mate.

Harp seals spend much of their time alone, swimming thousands of miles each year. But every winter, harp seals leave their ocean homes and move south to the sea ice. Here, male harp seals will fight each other to mate with females.

One male seal moves his flippers quickly across the ice. The fight begins! The first male strikes with his claws, while the other bites with sharp teeth. The winner is bloody but ready to claim his prize, a new mate. This may seem violent and harmful, but it is just another day during harp seal mating season!

Harp seals have sharp claws for fighting and capturing prey. ▶

HARP SEALS AT RISK

Harp seals belong to the family Phocidae. This family includes other earless seals. But harp seals are one of the most common. These 300-pound (135 kg) creatures are well adapted to the frigid waters of the Arctic.

While there are about 7.5 million harp seals in the world, the lives of harp seals are being threatened. Climate change is causing warmer temperatures and rapidly reducing sea ice in the Arctic. This lack of sea ice is affecting areas that harp seals call home, including Newfoundland, Greenland, and Russia.

Harp seals leave the oceans each year to have their babies. They use the thick, sturdy sea ice as a platform when giving birth and

WHAT IS CLIMATE CHANGE?

Climate change is periodic change in Earth's weather patterns. In recent years, scientists have observed an increase in the rate of climate change. Most scientists agree this is due to humans burning **fossil fuels**. Burning fossil fuels produces **greenhouse gases** which trap heat in Earth's atmosphere. This has led to rising global temperatures.

raising their young. Climate change is causing the sea ice to become too thin to support harp seals. Some areas don't have any sea ice.

This lack of strong sea ice is leading to fewer harp seal births. And fewer newly born harp seals survive. Without changes to stop climate change, new generations of harp seals may never be established.

HARP SEAL RANGE MAP

ASIA

ARCTIC OCEAN

EUROPE

◆
NORTH POLE

■ WHERE HARP
SEALS LIVE

NORTH AMERICA

ARCTIC ADAPTATIONS

It is usually cold in the Arctic. In the winter, the average temperature is −40 degrees Fahrenheit (−40°C). Arctic summers are short and the temperature is rarely higher than 50 degrees Fahrenheit (10°C).

Harp seals' bodies are made for living in cold conditions. Harp seals have fur and a thick layer of blubber. These help keep them warm and protect their bodies. The blubber also provides an additional energy source when seals don't have food to eat.

Harp seals have front and back flippers. These flippers help harp seals swim in the sea and move quickly across ice. To retain heat while resting on the ice, seals hold their front flippers close to their bodies. And they keep their back flippers pressed together. This exposes less of the seal's surface to the cold ice.

Harp seals' back flippers cannot rotate, so they only use their front flippers to move. A harp seal moves on land by dragging its body forward.

MATING AND BABIES

Breeding is a large part of life for harp seals. Harp seals start breeding when they are about five years old. Harp seals leave the water in the winter to mate. They gather in three large groups on sea ice near the coasts of Canada, Greenland, and Russia. In these areas, there may be as many as 2,000 seals per square mile (1.6 sq km)!

Harp seals then begin trying to attract mates. Male harp seals bark, wave their flippers, and chase females. Male seals will also fight each other to claim a female.

A female harp seal's pregnancy lasts more than 11 months. Pups are usually born between February and April. When it's time to give birth, female harp seals gather together on the sea ice. This thick ice provides a platform. It keeps the seals and their babies out of the water.

Each female harp seal gives birth to one pup. A harp seal pup weighs about 24 pounds (11 kg) at birth. It is covered in thick white fur. This helps insulate the pup because it does not have blubber

Harp seal pups are often called whitecoats because of their fluffy white fur.

yet. The white fur also helps baby seals blend in with their icy surroundings. This helps hide them from predators.

During the first two weeks of its life, the pup spends much of its time alone. The mother seal frequently leaves to hunt in the water.

To save energy, the pup mostly sits in one spot. When the mother seal returns, she can recognize her pup from its smell and the sound of its bark.

The pup nurses for 12 days. A female harp seal's milk has a lot of fat, so the pup grows quickly. A pup gains 4.4 pounds (2 kg) per day. It also grows a layer of insulating blubber. After a pup stops nursing, its mother leaves to mate again. The pup is on its own for good.

The seal pup soon sheds its white fur. It starts growing a spotted gray and black coat. The pup sits on the ice while it waits for its new coat to grow fully. It loses about half its weight during this time. After six weeks, the pup can swim and hunt for itself.

 Female harp seals touch noses with their babies to greet them.

LIFE IN THE ARCTIC

Once a harp seal is grown, it will spend most of its time alone swimming in the Arctic and north Atlantic Oceans. After breeding season, harp seals swim out to sea. They may travel 3,000 miles (4,828 km) each year!

Harp seals leave the water occasionally to rest. They stay on ice for longer periods when they are breeding and molting. Harp seals molt once a year in April or May. When on the sea ice, harp seals make holes in the ice. These holes let the seals enter the water quickly. They also provide places for the seals to surface and breathe while swimming under the ice.

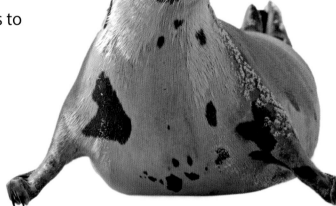

When harp seals gather to breed or molt, they communicate with each other.

While harp seals are on land, they often gather in large groups. These groups are called herds.

They do this with clicking, chirping, barking, and growling sounds. Harp seals make sounds underwater called underwater calls. While underwater, harp seals listen for other seals' calls and respond to them.

When in the water, seals spend a lot of time hunting. Harp seals mostly eat fish, including cod, halibut, and herring. They also eat crustaceans such as shrimp and krill. Harp seals can dive up to 1,200 feet (366 m) when hunting. They can stay underwater for 16 minutes.

Harp seals are aided by strong hearing when hunting underwater. And harp seals' whiskers can detect vibrations and movement. This helps harp seals find their prey. Harp seals also have sharp eyesight in both darkness and bright light. These features help harp seals become strong Arctic hunters.

While harp seals are predators, they are also prey. Harp seals must be on the lookout both in the water and on the ice. They are hunted by polar bears, orcas, walruses, sharks, and even humans.

 While harp seals spend most of their lives in water, they rarely drink it. They get most of the water they need from their food.

CHAPTER 6

HUNTING AND OVERFISHING

Throughout history, humans have been a major threat to harp seals. People have hunted them for their meat, skin, blubber, and fur. These body parts could be used for food, clothing, and oil.

Baby harp seals have been especially **vulnerable** to hunting. Their soft white fur was in high demand for coats and other clothing. Baby seal pelts could be sold for high prices.

Harp seals were hunted so extensively that their numbers **declined** rapidly. In the 1960s and 1970s, there were only 1.5 million harp seals in the world. Hunting has declined in recent years due to regulations. In most countries, hunters can only kill a certain number of harp seals each year. This has led to an increase in the global seal population.

The fishing industry also threatens harp seal populations. Fishing nets are often used in harp seal **habitats**. Seals can get trapped in these nets and die. Areas where harp seals live are also overfished. This greatly reduces harp seals' prey so they don't have enough to eat.

Nearly all seals killed by hunters in Canada are between three weeks and three months old.

EFFECTS OF CLIMATE CHANGE

While hunting and overfishing have caused seal populations to decline, the biggest threat to harp seals is climate change. Warmer temperatures have caused a rapid reduction in sea ice in the Arctic. Researchers at Duke University in North Carolina have studied the changes in sea ice in harp seal habitats. They found that sea ice in harp seal habitats has become 6 percent smaller per decade since 1979.

Sea ice is now nonexistent in many areas of the Arctic. Existing sea ice is often thin and melts quickly. Harp seals rely on sea ice for breeding and molting. The ice is especially important when female harp seals give birth to pups. The mothers require thick, solid ice so they can give birth safely.

Without sea ice, harp seals are forced to give birth in the water. Newborn harp seals cannot swim and therefore drown. If the mother seal gives birth on thin ice, the ice platform often breaks. The baby harp seal can be crushed by large pieces of ice.

Lack of suitable ice has caused the rate of survival for harp seal babies to decline sharply. In 2007, 75 percent of harp seal pups born in Canada died. In 2010, almost no harp seal pups survived. This means there are fewer adults to breed more harp seals. Without changes, new generations of harp seals will keep dying.

Climate change is also allowing more human interference in the lives of harp seals. A lack of sea ice has provided more open water

Harp seals require ice that is at least 12 to 28 inches (30 to 70 cm) thick.

for boats to travel on. Companies have begun sending ships into Arctic waters. Emissions from ships' engines can pollute the ocean. They can also hit and kill harp seals and other marine animals in the water.

Another threat to Arctic **habitats** is oil spills. Oil companies are interested in offshore drilling in the Arctic. Oil drilling comes with a risk of oil spills. It would be extremely difficult to clean up an oil spill in the Arctic. In fact, it would take several days for help to even arrive should an oil spill occur in the Arctic Ocean. By then it could be too late to prevent major damage.

Oil from an oil spill covers harp seals' fur and skin. This often causes death, especially for harp seal pups. After an oil spill near Canada in 1969, many dead harp seal pups washed ashore.

Increased tourism is affecting Arctic habitats. Cruise ships pollute the ocean and sometimes hit and injure marine animals.

CHAPTER 8

IMPORTANCE OF HARP SEALS

Experts think harp seals are unlikely to adapt to the changing climate of the Arctic. This will lead to increased harp seal pup deaths. Without baby harp seals, harp seal populations will decline.

With fewer harp seals, predators who eat them will have less food. These predators include species that are already threatened by climate change, such as polar bears. Predators will have to hunt other species. This could cause a reduction in species that would have been otherwise unaffected.

Harp seals are also predators. They provide balance in the Arctic ecosystem by managing prey abundance. In certain areas, including the Atlantic coast of Canada, seals are the largest predators. Without seals, the populations of small fish and other prey would rise. This would put the ecosystem out of balance.

Harp seals also offer more concrete benefits to their ecosystems. The feces of harp seals provide nutrients for the ecosystem, creating

Seals are the most common prey of polar bears.

a **cycle** of life. For example, seal **feces** help sea plants grow. The plants add oxygen to the water for fish to breathe. Then the seals eat the fish. This process makes the harp seal an important part of the Arctic ecosystem.

SAVING HARP SEALS

The International Union for the Conservation of Nature (IUCN) lists harp seals as Least Concern. This means the species as a whole is not considered endangered. However, that does not mean harp seals are not at risk.

IUCN

The International Union for the Conservation of Nature is a global authority on the **status** of wildlife. It collects scientific data and experts' studies to determine the status of a species. Then, governments and conservation organizations use this information to make decisions about species protection.

In the United States, harp seals are protected by the Marine Mammal Protection Act. This law established protections for marine wildlife. Similar laws exist in other countries, such as Canada. And more than 35 countries have banned the import of seal products.

Although seal hunting is allowed, demand has declined in recent years. Organizations such as the International Fund for

Organizations work to help injured harp seals. The seals are then released back into the wild when they recover.

Animal Welfare (IFAW) have worked to raise awareness of seal hunting. Education has shifted public opinion against seal hunting.

The IFAW, Sea Shepherd Conservation Society, and other organizations help raise awareness of climate change and habitat loss. These groups also support laws limiting greenhouse gas emissions. With education and new laws, many harp seals may be saved!

HARP SEAL
FACT SHEET

SCIENTIFIC NAME:
Pagophilus groenlandicus

LENGTH: 6 feet (1.8 m)

WEIGHT: 400 pounds
(181 kg)

DIET: carnivore

**AVERAGE LIFESPAN
IN THE WILD:** 20 years

IUCN STATUS: Least
Concern

WHAT CAN YOU DO?

You can take action to help harp seals and other Arctic animals at risk!

▷ Give money to or volunteer for harp seal conservation organizations, such as Oceana, the IFAW, and the Seal Conservation Society.

▷ Write to local lawmakers asking them to support policies that protect harp seals. These policies include laws that limit **greenhouse gas** emissions.

▷ Tell your friends and family about climate change and how it affects Arctic wildlife such as harp seals.

▷ Reduce your individual use of **fossil fuels** by choosing to bike, walk, or take the bus instead of riding in a car.

GLOSSARY

crustacean (kruhs-TAY-shuhn)—any of a group of animals with a hard shell and jointed legs. Crabs, lobsters, and shrimp are all crustaceans.

cycle—a period of time or a complete process that repeats itself.

decade—a period of ten years.

decline—to become lower in amount.

endangered—in danger of becoming extinct.

feces—solid bodily waste.

fossil fuel—a fuel formed in the earth from the remains of plants or animals. Coal, oil, and natural gas are fossil fuels.

frigid—very cold.

greenhouse gas—a gas, such as carbon dioxide, that traps heat in Earth's atmosphere.

habitat—a place where a living thing is naturally found.

halibut—a large fish that lives in the Atlantic and Pacific Oceans that is often eaten as food.

insulate—to keep something from losing heat.

krill—very small creatures that live in the ocean.

molt—to shed skin, hair, or feathers and replace with new growth.

nutrient—a substance that plants, animals, and people need to live and grow.

orca—a black-and-white whale species. Orcas are also called killer whales.

pregnancy—the condition of having one or more babies growing within the body.

shed—to cast off hair, feathers, skin, or other coverings or parts by a natural process.

shrimp—a small shellfish often caught for food.

status—a state or a condition.

vulnerable—able to be hurt or attacked. An animal has a vulnerable status when it is likely to become endangered.

whisker—one of the long hairs around the mouth of an animal.

INDEX